Bats in the Band

WRITTEN AND ILLUSTRATED BY **BRIAN LIES**

HOUGHTON MIFFLIN HARCOURT   BOSTON   NEW YORK

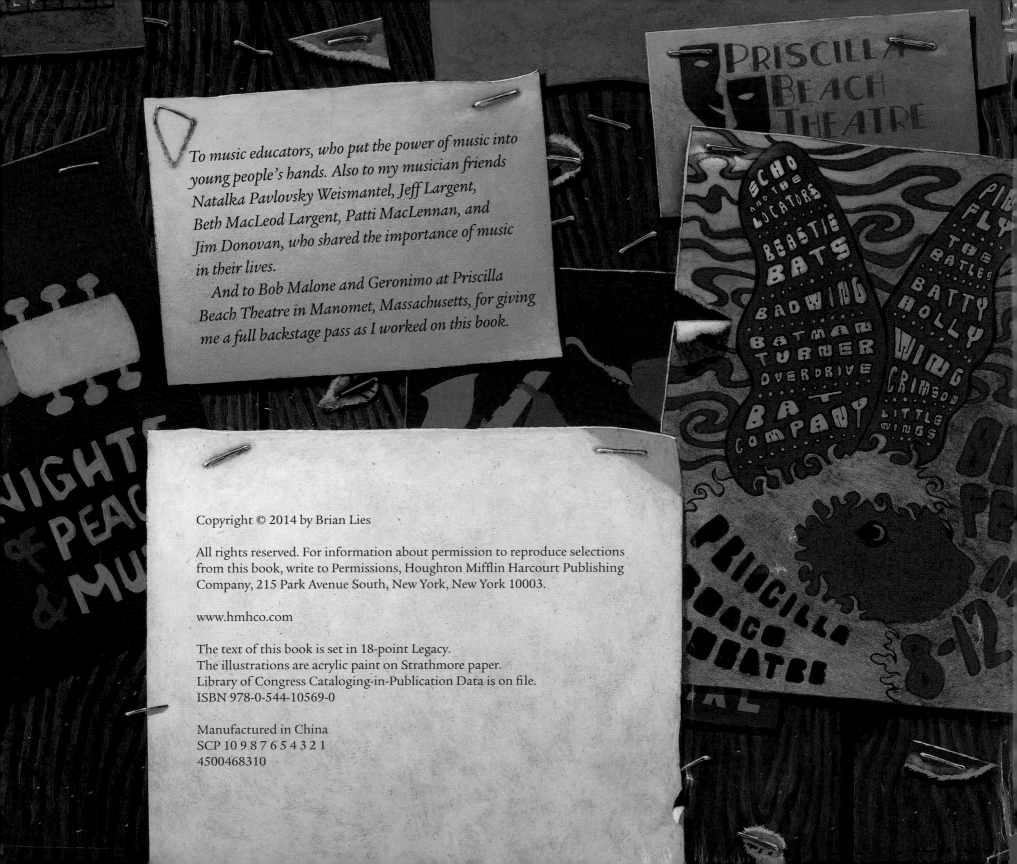

To music educators, who put the power of music into young people's hands. Also to my musician friends Natalka Pavlovsky Weismantel, Jeff Largent, Beth MacLeod Largent, Patti MacLennan, and Jim Donovan, who shared the importance of music in their lives.

    And to Bob Malone and Geronimo at Priscilla Beach Theatre in Manomet, Massachusetts, for giving me a full backstage pass as I worked on this book.

www.hmhco.com

The text of this book is set in 18-point Legacy.
The illustrations are acrylic paint on Strathmore paper.
Library of Congress Cataloging-in-Publication Data is on file.
ISBN 978-0-544-10569-0

Manufactured in China
SCP 10 9 8 7 6 5 4 3 2 1
4500468310

In hibernation we rest, asleep,
through icy months of storm,
        still . . .
                still . . .
                        huddled together,
and waiting for weather to warm.

But as the wicked winter thaws,
we stretch our wings and shake our claws.
Hunger drives us to the air.
We've got to eat. No time to spare!

We sing for our supper, in brightening mood.
Swooping and diving, we're finding our food.
There isn't a menu. We play it by ear,
chirping—and chasing the echoes we hear.

But each of us senses that something's not right.
And then when a bugle blast shatters the night,
that one lonely note tells us just what is wrong:
We're hungry for sound—we've been silent too long.

Relief on our faces is easy to read.
A little night music is just what we need!

And every last one of us knows where to go:
a summertime theater, after a show.
We're chasing each other. *Come on—look alive!*
Nobody wants to be last to arrive.

But as we approach it, there aren't any lights.
We can't be mistaken—we *know* it's tonight.
We circle above—then a window's thrown wide.
It lights up the lawn and it leads us inside.

We swoop through the window, ignoring the bats
offering T-shirts, posters, and hats.
A musical feast awaits us within . . .
Why would we stop? We can't wait to begin!

The space we fly into is warm and inviting.
We set up the stages and fiddle with lighting.

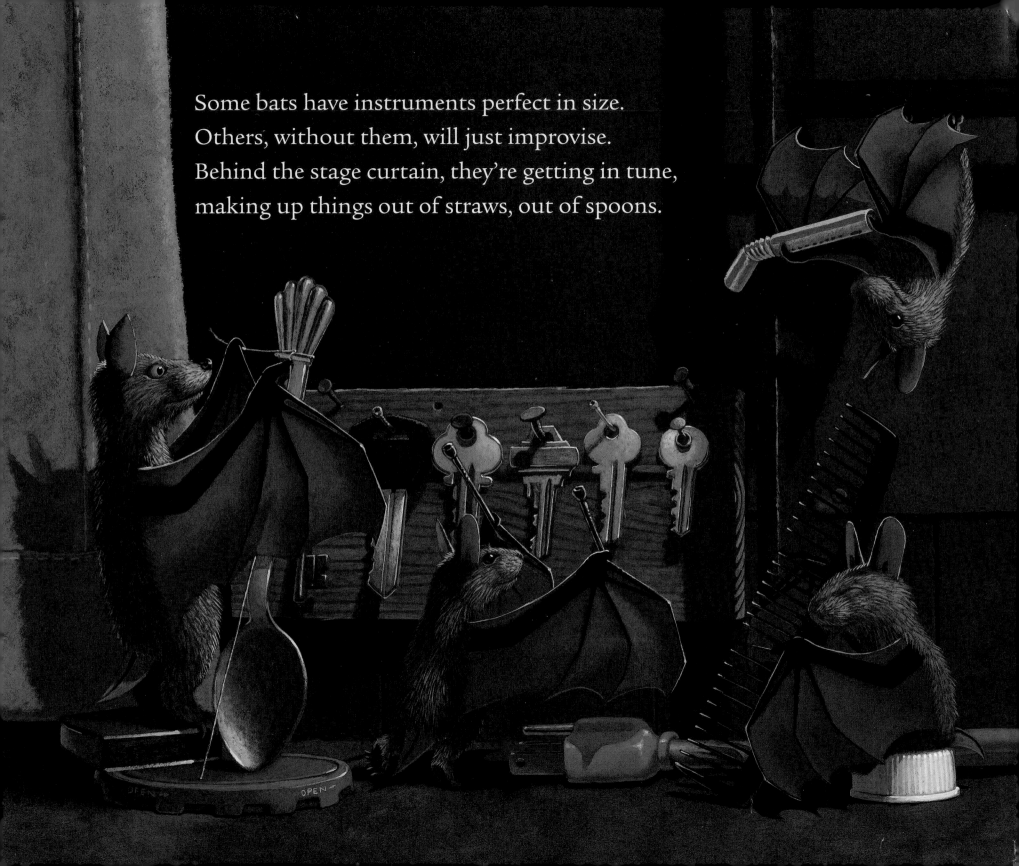

Some bats have instruments perfect in size.
Others, without them, will just improvise.
Behind the stage curtain, they're getting in tune,
making up things out of straws, out of spoons.

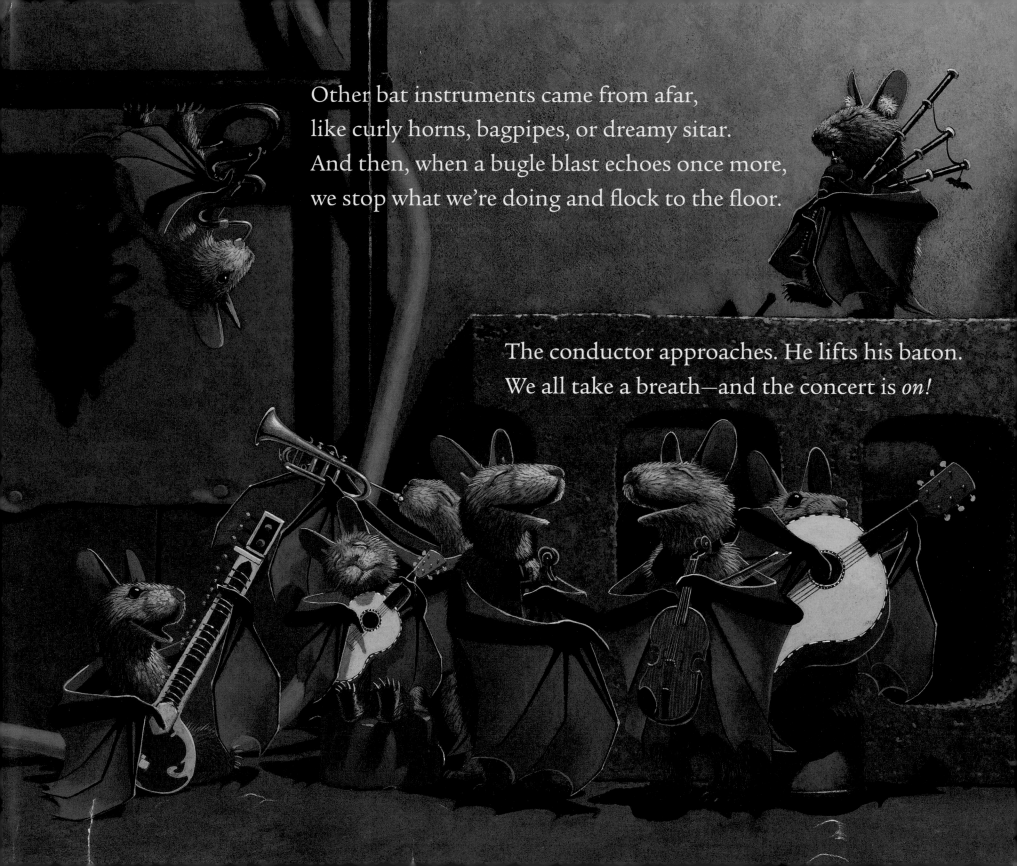

Other bat instruments came from afar,
like curly horns, bagpipes, or dreamy sitar.
And then, when a bugle blast echoes once more,
we stop what we're doing and flock to the floor.

The conductor approaches. He lifts his baton.
We all take a breath—and the concert is *on!*

We sing together as one voice.
It seems the very walls rejoice!
All together, rafters ringing . . .
it's as though our *souls* are singing.

Then violins, viola, cello,
change the mood to sweet and mellow.
If you haven't seen a bat quartet,
you really ain't seen *nothing* yet!

The one-bat band plays many things
at once, with feet and breath and wings.
And though we think this bat's inspired,
watching leaves us feeling . . . tired!

Next up, there's a country song—
some lonesome bat done someone wrong.
He's gone and broken someone's heart.
Now everything has come apart.

In a corner, tucked away
and far from where the others play,
there's something for the younger set
who can't sit through a concert yet.

Over there, a singer cries
of lonely days and empty skies.
Her feelings fill the room with blue
and soon we find we're crying too.

It's hard to figure—eyes get wetter,
. . . so how is it that we feel *better*?

Now on the main stage, there's a hum
of air guitar, and blazing drums.
Hearts are pumping, drums are thumping,
everything that's loose is jumping.

Can others hear us? We don't care!
Let our spirits fill the air!

Everybody joins the beat,
clapping wings and stomping feet.
We bounce, we hop, we twirl, we groove—
the music *makes* our bodies move.

But daylight through the windows says it's time for us to go,
so every bat who's willing crowds the stage to end our show.

The music soars. Finale's here, the ending of the song.

It builds and builds—
now here it comes!

It's going . . .

going . . .

Then the shimmering vibrations
dwindle down and fade away—
and a silence fills our ears,
as loud as anything we played.

A weary cheer—there's nothing more, but no one wants to leave.
Our music was a gift we gave, and one that we received.
But finally we've got to go. We stretch and wave goodbye.
Worn out, wrung out, half asleep, we greet the morning sky.

Heading for home, we hum or we sing,
and discover there's music in *everything*:
the roar of a car, or the bark of a pup—
the sound of the rest of the world waking up.

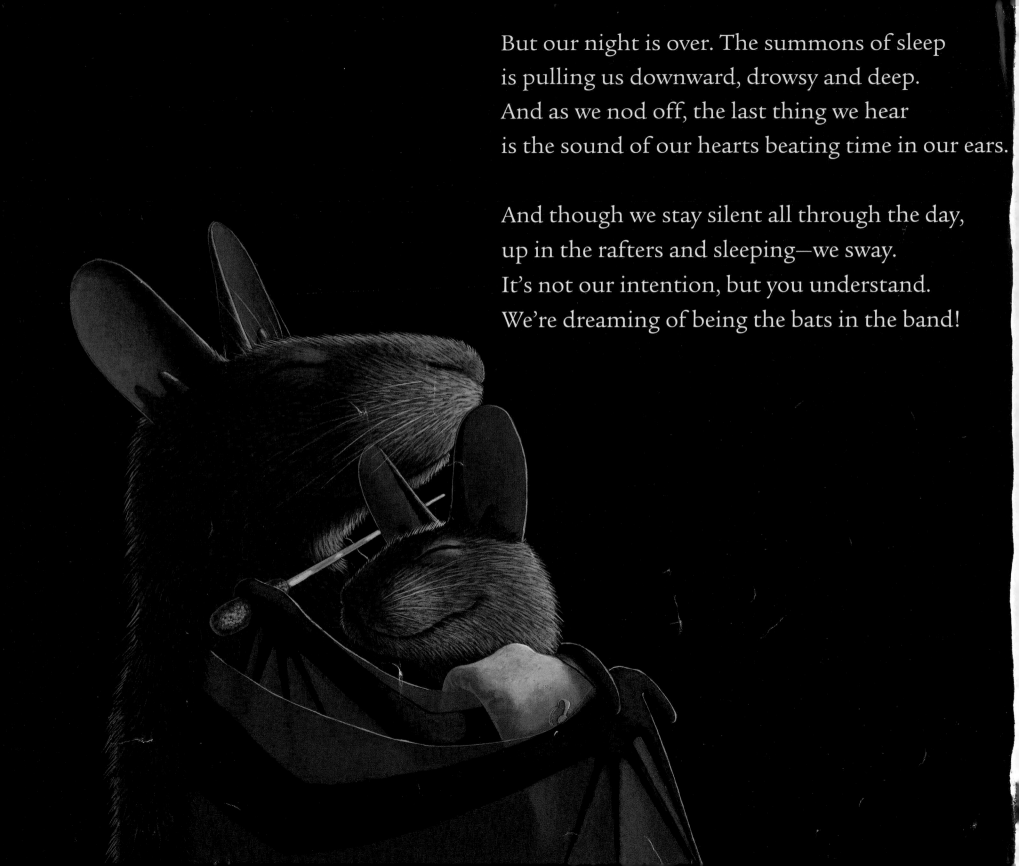

But our night is over. The summons of sleep
is pulling us downward, drowsy and deep.
And as we nod off, the last thing we hear
is the sound of our hearts beating time in our ears.

And though we stay silent all through the day,
up in the rafters and sleeping—we sway.
It's not our intention, but you understand.
We're dreaming of being the bats in the band!